RUTH FINNEGAN

PEARL OF THE WIND

THE KATE-PEARL ROMANCE SERIES: THREE

First Edition 2023

PEARL OF THE WIND

ISBN 978-1-739-89370-5

Published by Callender Press 2023

First Edition 2023

Callender Press | callenderpress.co.uk | Milton Keynes

United Kingdom

Covers, design, layout and production by John Hunt at mapperou.com

PEARL OF THE WIND

The Poet-of-the-Aire sings the Lay of the Lady Catherine
of Olden Time
as heard one dawn by mortal ears
in dreams
and told forth as commanded me
in the wing-ed words of the spirit's breath-ed psyche
here
by the handmaiden Ruth in the olden breath of breathing

A romance novel by Ruth Finnegan

On a Day
When the wind is perfect
THE SAIL
JUST NEEDS TO OPEN
AND THE WORLD IS
FULL OF BEAUTY.
Today
IS such a Day.
Rumi

"On a day when the wind is perfect,
the sail just needs to open and the world is full of beauty.

Today is such a day.
My eyes are like the sun that makes promises;
the promise of life that it always
keeps each morning.

The living heart gives to us
Like that luminous sphere,
both caress the earth with tenderness.
This is a breeze that can enter the soul.
This love I know plays a drum.

Arms move around me;
who can contain their pelf before my beauty?
Peace is wonderful,
but ecstatic dance is more fun,
less narcissistic;
gregarious He makes our lips.

On a day when the wind is perfect,
the sail just needs to open
and the love starts".

Rumi

"Blow blow
thou winter wind
thou art not so unkind
As man's ingratitude".
Thy tooth is not so keen,
Because thou art not seen,
Although thy breath be rude.
Heigh-ho! sing, heigh-ho! unto the green holly:
Most friendship is feigning, most loving mere folly:
Then, heigh-ho, the holly!
This life is most jolly.

William Shakespeare

CONTENTS

RUTH FINNEGAN
The Black Inked Pearl
THE KATE-PEARL SERIES: BOOK ONE

PEARL
OF THE
SEAS

THE
HELIX
PEARL
THE STORY OF THE
WINE DARK GARRULOUS SEA
RUTH FINNEGAN

Hearing
Others
Voices
LISTEN TO THIS
the astounding ups and downs
“ of quotation marks ”
Ruth Finnegan
“ABOUT four in the morning! ſays the ill-
“natured reader,——What then were you
“doing till that hour——with an opera-dancer,
“a fille-de-joye?” To which I anſwer literally,
Nothing. “No!——Mr. Yorick, the impoſiti-
“on is too groſs to paſs upon us even from the
“pulpit. What did you do with the gands
Continued on back cover

First Note

A myth is for centuries, maybe forever. It may spawn a thousand tales but in essence remain the same. The oft-told myth of the young girl rejecting her love in fear, then seeking him through all space, recycles again and again across the world and over the centuries.

So it is with this tale. It is at root the same tale as in the earlier Kate-Pearl stories *The Black Inked Pearl* and its prequel *Voyage of Pearl of the Seas,* as well as in the later story told by the sea, *The Helix Pearl.* But this time it is from a different perspective – that of our call to the fleeting flighting breathing air, the soul, the fluttering butterfly-psyche.

More, the style is the same. Again, you will find – but need not precisely identify – plentiful literary allusions (a process more fully explored in my *Listen to this: the astounding ups and downs of quotation marks*); most are just hints, but passages in double quote marks are direct quotations; other poems and the like are from Kate's own imagination transmitted here through her earthly interlocutor Ruth.

As Ruth I found these allusions unavoidable rather than arising from deliberate conscious choice. Some of them swam up from texts learned long ago, by heart, at my Quaker school, others from the long steeped-in literature and mythology of the ancient world, my university study, above all from Homer, poet of poets, who returns again and again. For him too perhaps – here as throughout our lives, air-born metaphors emerge from the sounding airwaves of his mind.

Only some of these many allusions are annotated in the Author's Notes at the end of the book. Some readers – not everyone – may find these of interest. The rest are left to my readers/listeners, if they so choose (you may not wish to, it is not needful), to winkle out.

The story's origin in dreams – that is, in the magical space between sleeping and waking – means that some episodes are elusive. To me too. I can only say that I wrote them as I heard and felt them in their (to me unexpected and unsought) dreaming mode. I found that I had no choice but to write them down the next day, as accurately as I could, in faith that a meaning was there, intended. Perhaps you will detect it better than I. For me it was a kind of dictation from a source outside myself (and for once this is not a metaphor, a familiar trope in literature, but a felt, literal, reality).

Till it was written down I never forgot. But once there on the page I had no memory of anything but the overall story and, above all, the *feel*. I suggest that, as with poetry or epic, you might like to read it the same way – for the overall themes and feeling – and the *sound* – not forever worrying about the literal detail.

The book was written in three magical days on a sea journey, looking out on the enchantment of clouds, sunrise and sunset, a time for the liminal in-between mystical place of dream. Since then I have added some small revisions and elucidations, but the basic story is unchanged.

No doubt there are still (I am only human) some 'mis-writes' and infelicities: anyway, who in this human world of ours can agree on the best style? I would be glad, however, if you could note that some, hopefully all, of the at-first-sight wrong spellings, grammar or punctuation, and the scattering of unusual words, are not typos but there for the sake of *the sound and the rhythm*, essential features in this dream-steeped narrative.

It is set out as prose and until I read it aloud that is how I might have described it and allowed my computer to treat it. But in fact I suspect that my unthinking unconscious, my feeling-imagination, knew better all along and had already flown the text into pulse-beaten wing-ed words.

And if that, dear reader, sounds pretentious – to me too – I can only say, again, that that is how it came: I tell it as it was heard.

I think if you too read it aloud and pause to feel the sounding words and the rhythms, you too might wonder if much of it is more of poetry than of prose, and, like all poems, echo-ridden and soaked in repetition (actually I should have known this all along, for I had found the same thing in turn with all the earlier Kate-Pearl stories too; perhaps, do you think, with poetry you have to discover it afresh each time?)

So when in doubt think of this as mostly a kind of poetry, and if you will be so kind, speak it aloud.

Kate together with her earthly intermediary (me) sometimes likes to use Anglo Saxon/Teutonic endings, as in *-en* (often but not always for a plural) or *-es* (genitive – the abbreviated form is, now, written as 's),

also at times old spellings or unconventional but understandable word orders when she feels they sound better and more rhythmic. It is the same with the extensions, separations and abbreviations of words. These sonic and poetic dimensions, let me repeat, and the homeric word associations too, are an integral dimension of the tale.

For example when Kate – or the Poet of the Aire – says, or, rather, sings "sweeten" rather than "sweet" it is because the line then flows more rhythmic and sweet. For those willing to listen it can add depth to the meaning too. The "sweeten" wasn't deliberate or thought-out, it just *felt* to be the right way of saying it. I take it that it was a way of *intensifying* the word so it conveyed that some thing (love often enough) was *very* sweet, sweetest. And then again it spread wider into being both – as you read or, if you like, *hear* it – an active *and* a passive adjective: in other words meaning that the thing had been, and perhaps was still being, sweetened, made sweet, or was itself actively sweeten*ing*, maybe sweetening everything all around. I think that perhaps those old (maybe I mean olden) meanings of "sweeten" somehow floated into my mind. And so with other, similar, adjectives.

Again the ending *-es* gives (to me anyway) an implication not just of the possessive but the feel, somehow, of an ancient almost mediaeval poetry and for that reason in some way, in some near-mystical magical time, in keeping with world of the Ancient Poet's Lay.

'New' (but maybe old) words and spellings and runs of sonic associations have the same foundation. They are a play with language, allowed, it seems to poets and verbal artists – I remember Gerald Manley Hopkins' resonant sonic-echoing poetry, or James Joyce and William Faulkner. Dante and Shakespeare too (not that in any earthly sense I am comparing myself to *them*). This feature, a cause of offence to literal readers, is possibly slightly less prominent than in *The Black Inked Pearl* but, as in that story, the style, sonic and rhythmic, goes by feel rather than convention, oral and spontaneous rather than written. After all who looks up the dictionary or the grammar book when speaking or telling a love story? This tale, as I say, is, like children's stories, best read aloud – then any unusual syntax and vocabulary will fall into place.

Language is after all so very wonderful, so many-layered, so redolent of ancient insights, so entwined with the listeners' felt, and differing, creative interpretations.

To go back to the book's central theme, the air, the atmosphere – once started I was amazed how much this enters into our metaphors, our poetry, our science (much of this quite new to me), even into our common language. So I have taken the liberty of expanding our vision of the Poet with a touch of science (I spare you the equations). This I hope may be accepted not as padding or as show-off knowledge but as a way of deepening, a little, our imaginative grasp on this pervasive, unseen, constituent of life.

This, then, oh reader, is again a tale of love and its eternal existence, moulded by mythic fairytale memories and by the riddling between dream and reality. And many tales in one. I hope you enjoy this different version, told in the main not in the singular third person, as often in *The Black Inked Pearl* and *Voyage of the Pearl of the Seas,* or the first as in the *Helix Pearl*'s voice of the garrulous wine-dark sea, but pervaded by the second, a call to the breathing breath-ed ever-present air.

It may not be the last, for still to sing to you are the plural 'they' of fire's flames, then – ... (well, we will see). For why should the air, the clouds, the breath, for all their power, have the last word?

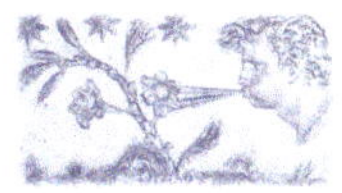

The Invocation

Sing to me now Great Poet of the Winds, sing of the wrath of deepen breathing-thinking hero in the skies wind-sweeten-swepten there.

Sing of the wandering of his best-belov-ed Kate, the fearful frighten' braven one, and of her flightsome quest through the air-clad sounding universe.

Sing on, dear Aire-held Poet, my inspirati-on one,

So now in wind of air, in mother of storms and whirls and spurling scrolls of sea (yes she the sea has her story too, but other where, and you are older still than her), speak on!

Sing of love lost and maybe found.

Sing of the toils and moils and spoils of destiny. And moons to rise and fall again. And human per-sev-erancing.

Of God who reigns above even you, the wind, the air, who gathers the breath of living creatures all.

Sing me of *love*.

Sing of that love reject'd on Irish shore, sore Donegal wind that thunder owns, by wild waves shook, oh ye who rule the sea and all its beings.

For is it not love that comes in the breath, the pulsing breathing lungs, the soul, the spiritus, the very seat and feel of life.

Sing of today. Or long ago. Of the gasping gusting panic of her heart, afraid, afraid of love, and not yet skilled.

Sing in the sighing of the wind, sobs of the breeze that moves the trees, sing me of that love again and yet again. Even so of your grace that I may hear, and know it true.

Sing of the seagull cries in her winding hair, the long dark hair he loved, flown tossed and tangled in your gusts, your breath.

So then again I call and plead with you

Breathe breathe now, sing to me

Oh wind blow through my soul

Oh air uplift, sustain

Spirit of all Spirits, breath, espiritus, efflatus that is the light and soul of me, divine.

and interfuses all,

Wing me your voiced entrancing song

Onward then onward go, ye winds,

and blow!

Prologue

And so as I breathed and prayed to her, Great Spirit of the Aire, the winds around behinden me, I felt them, singing swinging bringing the song.

Not my song it was, but *yours.*

Yes yours it is, breathed winged and called in invocationing the breathing of meditat-ion.

Not my singing. Hers, the wind's, the singing ever wind-es song.

Harken then, harken well ye mortals now, breathe to her singing, breathe 't in your innermost soul. Hush, she is here.

The Beginning

It was in those old days, oh sacred breath of breaths I hear you say, that one day a young girl, walking on a shore in the mystery-filled misty myth-ful many-sea-gulled Celtic lands of yore, once lost her breath. And panicked there.

You saw. It was from his arms she panic-fled. In mist. His head was bending down to her, his breath was in her mouth, ready to –

No!

Bending towards her, breath from his curving lips, nostrils a-rounding her.

Well then? How did that sweet life go (or mine?) on that many-sea-gulled Irish shore? Sing me of that, Great Spirit now,

Sing of the wind-blown sounds, crash through the air, clouds in the sky above in the breath of winds, the breath of love.

Sing of the mountains purple clothed, in clouded swirl.

Sing of the sea, its depths, its hidden beings, birds, its shells and surges quiet and wild.

'No no', you heard her say, Great Spirit Poet, and told to me, 'No no, I am too young ... too young to breathe his breath, to feel the winds of heaven blow us both togethering'.

So sad, you say.

So, run away, gasp-heaving breath. Her gasping, running, panic, running running, catchen, going, breath ...

'Oh girl', you cried, 'Oh do not fear nor flee. It is only him, the very soul of love, the air you breathe. What there to fear?'

But she – she'd fled.

Fearing the very air of life, the place to breath.

Running away.

And from there, oh wind, oh voice that's ever in my ears, is the story come. The story of a girl in the wind.

Of Kate. Who was afraid.
You saw it all.

Girl in the Winds

Tell me again oh Thou of the Air, the Wind, Sing of the girl, of Kate, whose tale was not yet told. Of a man of wrath and cunning wile, the one that loved. And was reject.

You saw. You saw the mists of that many-sea-gulled shore 'cross which she fled. In olden time.

An ordinary girl she was. In a magick'd world.

She would sit silent there, feeling the clouds, the sky, numbering the moons of Jupiter, fires of the stars. The winds of heaven. She leaped and sang as she flew through heather-scented fragrant air, blown sound from storm-driven waves, fighting 'n delight the headstrong wind.

Ah, joy it was to be alive.

You saw, did not forget.

The Wind-es Arts

It was not enough, that joy, even in those olden days of time before.

Now must she go, inquiring, to the great north-windes back. To that great school for her beginning to grow.

And there she learnt – ?

Forgive me oh Goddess, that I do not know. Hear me, oh graciously hear me, instruct me of thy great wisdom in this hour.

I bow my head and hear. And as I hear so do I speak.

How the beginning was. The end. And the places of the winds.

Of these she learned – that young girl Kate, as you tell it me in song.

So, in the sighing silent sounding soughing voices of the wind she heard that (solemn now) –

That it's taken four and a half billion years for the emergence of human life on earth. Even before the sun and its planets were formed, the early stars transmitted oxygen transmuted into carbon and the other atoms – ten billion years.

That the size of the universe is the distance travelled by life since the Big Bang. And so the present visible universe is ten billion light-years across.

Is that not miracle?

So unimportant are you dear Kate, even you, in the cosmic scheme of things. All come in that long event chain shot through with cosmic spatial winds back back before our solar system grew, before the human race was born.

'But but', asked Kate, 'the start, the very start? how did that … … ?'

'Remember gravity, dear child, that makes the apples fall and holds the moon and planets in their paths. Holds too the galaxies till black holes' fateful force ...'

'Yes, yes?' – thus breathless Kate – ' what then, oh tell me truly now... '

'A mystery too far my child, Think only this. That at the beginning of things, the universe was squeezed and held within the size of an atom, quantum fluctuation could shake the universe, the whole of it.

'But as to what unifies the very large and very small – to understand what's going on, we cannot answer that. No, not. As yet. The mystery, even for solar cosmic winds, remains – of what was there before the far beginning then. Mayhap the empty unrelenting air of space'.

Amazing yes, but Kate, the eager wind-borne one, was not yet satisfied. Distracting-ness, best of all child-ward skills, we know it well – came into play,

"Would you not learn of the winds themselves?' you said, 'the truest ones of earth and heaven?'

'I know that well', Kate said, in sulk, 'they're always 'gainst me when I walk'.

'But each one sep-arate?'

Silence.

'Well Kate, Which one to start?'
'Oh – east. Get 't over with' (for an Irish girl east is the worst).
'Listen you then and hark it well'.

"The glorious East wind howls through the trees
It brings man's nature to its knees
The spirits of fortune ride through the air
offering childhood adventure to those who dare

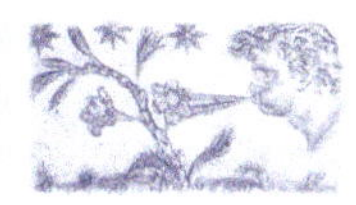

Oh, powerful wind, the music of my tossing soul
rage upon my mind as my heart needs control
Bellow loudly without a demon's care
for in the treetops, my life sails there
Oh, East wind I fear not your Hellish roar
for you lift my heart and let it soar
Surely from Heaven's gate you descend
to cleanse the spirit and let it mend".

'And, and, the north?' (that fiercest too. In Donegal).
'Well, if you must, you air-en girl.

"I love you, malcontent
Male wind—
Shaking the pollen from a flower
Or hurling the sea backward from the grinning sand.
Blow on and over my dreams...
Scatter my sick dreams...
Throw your lusty arms about me...
Envelop all my hot body...
Carry me to pine forests—
Great, rough-bearded forests...
Bring me to stark plains and steppes...
I would have the North to-night—
The cold, enduring North.
And if we should meet the Snow,
Whirling in spirals,
And he should blind my eyes...
Ally, you will defend me—
You will hold me close,
Blowing on my eyelids".

'West?' (all Irish girls just love that one do they not?)
'Not as sweet as you think dear Kate. But listen still'.

"O wild West Wind, thou breath of Autumn's being,
Thou, from whose unseen presence the leaves dead
Are driven, like ghosts from an enchanter fleeing,

Yellow, and black, and pale, and hectic red,
Pestilence-stricken multitudes: O thou,
Who chariotest to their dark wintry bed
The wingèd seeds, where they lie cold and low,
Each like a corpse within its grave, until
Thine azure sister of the Spring shall blow
Her clarion o'er the dreaming earth, and fill
(Driving sweet buds like flocks to feed in air)
With living hues and odours plain and hill:
Wild Spirit, which art moving everywhere;
Destroyer and Preserver; hear, O hear!
Thou on whose stream, 'mid the steep sky's commotion,
Loose clouds like Earth's decaying leaves are shed,
Shook from the tangled boughs of Heaven and Ocean,

Angels of rain and lightning: there are spread
On the blue surface of thine airy surge,
Like the bright hair uplifted from the head
Of some fierce Maenad, even from the dim verge
Of the horizon to the zenith's height,
The locks of the approaching storm. Thou dirge
Of the dying year, to which this closing night
Will be the dome of a vast sepulchre
Vaulted with all thy congregated might
Of vapours, from whose solid atmosphere
Black rain, and fire, and hail will burst: O hear!

Thou who didst waken from his summer dreams
The blue Mediterranean, where he lay,
Lulled by the coil of his crystalline streams,

Beside a pumice isle in Baiae's bay,
And saw in sleep old palaces and towers
Quivering within the wave's intenser day,
All overgrown with azure moss and flowers
So sweet, the sense faints picturing them! Thou
For whose path the Atlantic's level powers
Cleave themselves into chasms, while far below
The sea-blooms and the oozy woods which wear
The sapless foliage of the ocean, know
Thy voice, and suddenly grow grey with fear,
And tremble and despoil themselves: O hear!

If I were a dead leaf thou mightest bear;
If I were a swift cloud to fly with thee;
A wave to pant beneath thy power, and share

The impulse of thy strength, only less free
Than thou, O Uncontrollable! If even
I were as in my boyhood, and could be
The comrade of thy wanderings over Heaven,
As then, when to outstrip thy skiey speed
Scarce seemed a vision; I would ne'er have striven
As thus with thee in prayer in my sore need.
Oh! lift me as a wave, a leaf, a cloud!
I fall upon the thorns of life! I bleed!
A heavy weight of hours has chained and bowed
One too like thee: tameless, and swift, and proud.

Make me thy lyre, even as the forest is:
What if my leaves are falling like its own!
The tumult of thy mighty harmonies

Will take from both a deep, autumnal tone,
Sweet though in sadness. Be thou, Spirit fierce,
My spirit! Be thou me, impetuous one!

Drive my dead thoughts over the universe
Like withered leaves to quicken a new birth!
And, by the incantation of this verse,
Scatter, as from an unextinguished hearth
Ashes and sparks, my words among mankind!
Be through my lips to unawakened Earth
The trumpet of a prophecy! O Wind,
If Winter comes, can Spring be far behind?"

Ah that was good, So sweeten dear-en place, of breathing deep, of dreams and sleep, eternity.

'What then? Tis finished now, those many windes' ways'.
'Have you forgot? Then listen now'.

'Is it the south, sweet south-from wind', asked Kate , 'the last and best?'

"Where have you been, South Wind, this May-day morning,
With larks aloft, or skimming with the swallow,
Or with blackbirds in a green, sun-glinted thicket?

Oh, I heard you like a tyrant in the valley;
Your ruffian haste shook the young, blossoming orchards;
You clapped rude hands, hallooing round the chimney,
And white your pennons streamed along the river.

You have robbed the bee, South Wind, in your adventure,
Blustering with gentle flowers; but I forgave you
When you stole to me shyly with scent of hawthorn".

'Yes, all very nice' said Kate politely.
'And then -'
'No more' said Kate 'too long. And poetry – what use is that?'
'The inspiration of our inspirationing? It will be of use'.

So that was that. Was done. Her lesson ended now.

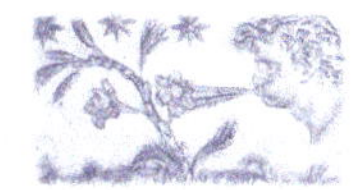

Oh Typhoon Blast!

Yes that was that, move on! Tell now Great Aerial Poet mine what came there next. To her?

You're silent still?

Did you go Africkward for story wise that blew her mind? Blast'd through her heart? Revolutioned her?

Ah yes. For who can recount the sudden strike, the typhoon blast? Of love, the love that sudden came for Kate? That lightning strike, fragrance of the beloved through the air!

Oh tell it not, that sacred mystery. That joy once known and ne'er forgot. That bitter bitterest gasping for that joy-reject', the guilt, the indrawn breath.

Oh typhoon, cyclones hurricane-in-hurricanes-n-hurriconings, more.

We cannot tell it here. Only the quest to come.

Alas for Kate, that hardest quest, love found too late. Alas.

Spire of the Windens' Magic Spiralling Air

Where should she search, I ask, oh singer mine?

> 'Where but that place of learning great, spires in the wind, minds free to the gusting air of heaven. Where all do search, all quests accepted there'.
>
> 'To find her love', I whispered to myself...

You heard. 'Who knows?', you said.

And so Kate came, afeard, but came.

Then came a thousand years of instant time. Time that he, hurt to death, forgave (perhaps he did – or feigning maybe for better punishment. Of Kate). A miracle if it were true.

He took her to the highest spire of all.

> 'Look round', he said 'and be not thou amazed with any great amazement my dear heart, my sweetest breath, but scent you here the fragrance of sweet ever-love. And wisdom too. Eternity. And do you still keep faith, have faith. So now see power. The test'.

Then leaped he from that highest tower. Kate watched aghast.

For the angels missed. He dashed his head against the stones.

And died. It seem-ed true.

The Quest Begun

Death! So she must seek him there, in Hades place, in hell? Or heaven perhaps was best? To pass the test he set – of love, of truth.

By now she knew her love, her ever love (*he* saw it not, was hard, the tale, her quest)l

High in the sky, you tell me Goddess mine, there must she go to finden him?

I listen, then I ask again, hard urging her to reply to me.

> 'And love? there to find love? in the upper air that men call heaven? 'tis true? '

She hesitated. 'Don't ask too much', she said 'just listen well. The Song of Kate and Him'.

> 'Does she find him, does she does she?' – persistent I – 'oh does she there? And has he forgiv'n that panic run? And let her be her, for her herself'?
>
> 'I told you, wait and hear. You want too much. She must still prove her love. Not quick or easy that. For any mortal one. Be still and hear thou it for now 'The Lay of Him and Kate', resounding in Sound and Ayre around the Universe. Then might you know'.

Of Air and Atmosphere

But there was more t'learn to help her quest, to get her there, to seek him true. Above. For how could Kate fond her belove'd if knowing not the way? Knowing not the very air that held him fast, that veiled his face, now far above?

Sing of that now oh muse that of your mercy I may know.

And here is what I heard, in mortal speech. Not good enough for those sweet sounds from immortal breath-ed voice, but 't must suffice for now.

Around the earth is *atmosphere*, the layer of gases called the *air*, surrounding all the planet Earth, retain-ed there by Earth-es gravitie.

The Blue Marble:* an image of Earth taken on December 7, 1972, by the Apollo 17 crew Harrison Schmitt and Ron Evans from a distance of about 29,000 kilometers (18,000 miles) from the planet's surface.*

OF AIR AND ATMOSPHERE

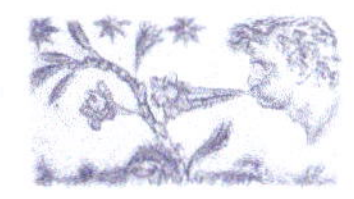

The atmosphere that protects all life on Earth. Creating pressure there for liquid water to exist on Earthes surfacing, absorbing ultraviolet solar radiationing, warming the surfaces in greenhouse heat, reducing temperature twixt day and night.

Dry air has – hear it now – much nitrogen and oxygen, of argon, carbon dioxide, yes, and other gases too. There is water vapour there, most at the level of the sea, and 0.4% over the whole atmosphere. Air composition, temperature, and atmospheric pressure too, varying with altitude. And air for use in photosynthesis by plants – a miracle again – and breathing animals, found only in Earth's troposphere and artificial atmospheres.

How solemn, literal, it was, But through all this must she now go forth.

And more.

And more again.

Sing her to winging, swinging, wondering, wandering, floundering there, so wing her through dear Goddess mine, Sing of your grace.

> "Let the beasts their breath resign,
> Strangers to the life divine;
> Who their God can never know,
> Let their spirit downward go".
> No poetry now ...

And know ye well, the atmosphere has a great mass of three quarters nearer to the surface. The atmosphere gets thinner with increasing altitude, no definite boundary between the atmosphere and outer space.

Oh now again oh sing me, breath of love.

> "For this
> – accepted Breath –
> Through it
> – compete with Death".

So Kate. She must face all. Must go into and through the danger-full upper air. To find him there.

And still must learn, stern goddess, teacher, again to learn, of this song too.

"I draw sweet air
Deeply and long,
As pure as prayer,
As sweet as song".

And then – and this is miracle too – of Earth, so harken now again again:

Atmospheric effects see them during atmospheric reentry of spacecraft 70 miles up. Many layers are there in the atmosphere, of temperatures and compositions.

She then sought for a poem again that was good, to carry her.
"In the dark of the night with you
alone in thought...do you ever wonder, if
when your last breath is drawn, there will
be more than life?"
Yet more, She paused and thought

"I did not know
In which train you went;
But my deep breath
Brought your train back".

Oh panicked gasping breath. Entrained t'ward space unknown. To upward go, go after him, to leave the Earth.

But go must she.

That too must she learn for at last to find-en him,

So up and upwards dearest Kate, go onwards further further on your quest. Through air and cloud and atmosphere now go. Alone. Afraid.

Through the unknown.
To space.

The Going Gone

Now million million miles gone up.

And now still upward more, no down to earth again, no easy earthen cliff near where she'd ran, on that many-sea-gulled shore, escaping him. But this time now – for *finding* him. She hoped.

Afraid afraid.
Afraid.
Twas outer space, no human mortals' home.
And yes, a voice through air.
Was him?
Was him?
Oh oh. Was *found!*

Embarking on a ship he was. Space ship. She saw him there.

The next? *Distancing*! Oh no –

Oh oh. To sail away.

'Oh wait, oh wait, I'm here, wait wait for me'

But you the cruel wind, oh testing one, you blew her wordings back, away from him (or perhaps he *would* not hear ...).

She ran, she ran, fast as that once escaping time, no, faster still she *hurled* herself against the holding wind,

'I'm here, I'm here, oh wait for me'.

But the ship – –

Run. Stumble. Reach out. No no, ship slipping away. It's going, going. Wind in sails, billowing, blowing blasting off in billowing wind.

Ju- – ust snatch rope-end.

She struggled, struggled, strained and reined, sprained stained her heart her hand her limbs, held on; cut her right hand she would she would she would.

But the rope of his boat, his dear boat, his dear body slipping swimming slimmening shimmering spinning – oh winning, dimming, grinning away from her fingers, the breaking broken shatterance.

Gone.

Gone with the wind.

Would he look back? The moon went behind a cloud (oh tale of her life) and hid his look. She could not see him. Shadowed. Vanishing.

Oh sparkling sea,
Oh empty bed,
Sunrise of beauty, and lone sunset red.
Ships aparting to far-off sands,
no heed to voices
or stretching hands
Rope slipping from fingers,
rough fibre on hands,
that are pulling and gripping,
fumbling and rasping,
struggling and nipping,
twisting and slipping,
fading and grasping
going and holding
and going and going
and holding and –
It was gone.

Gone in the shriek of the wind, the seagulls' cries, he was gone...

Another Song

But then Great Singer you sang another song. Harken to it now, it was for *her.* For Kate-es very self.

So, quiet now ye airway spirits, denizens of space above, that he is gone.

> Now you have holpen me
> and whispered in my ear
> 'Oh wait oh wait onlie, my dear
> for the ships that parted in the night
> will sail for ever near.

In the Sea's Wind Dance

Well yes, Kate thought, poetry's very well but – he was still gone.

She prayed then, how she prayed. Never before. Never before talked straight with you, my muse. Never before had she'd need of it.

And so you harked and answered unto her.

> 'To find him dear child? The road is long, oh long and long, and the wind, myself, hard in your face. Many years and centuries of human breaths'.

> 'I will find him' she said, 'whatever the song you sing, I *will*!'

> Sap of my sap
> and my soul's breath
> silk strands round maypole blown
>
> on tree of life
> my love
> my own.

You smiled at her naïveté (I saw) but still were a little moved.

> 'Well now, my dear, three tests. If you agree. Then may you fly upwards, still more up, to the upperest thinnest air of all, in search of him'.

Kate hesitated, fearful. Higher and higher still? Then firmly answered she your words.

> 'I do. I will'.

It is not hard my dear. Sing of three winds that I will name. *My* choice'.

Ah! That for Kate was easy. Well had she learned and set them deep, deep in her heart,

> 'Now first, the west'.

Kate sang.

> 'And now – you see I make it easiest, your favourite – south'.

Kate sang.

> 'And now th' most loved of all, south-west'.

> 'B-but but that is not a wind, not a proper ...'

You smiled.

'Not on the curriculum, not', cried Kate.

'No?'

'*Four* winds, just four, everyone knows that, *four*'.

'It was. Curriculumward, *was* there. You did not wait to learn it all.

Your quest is at an end. Go home'.

Kate wept and wept and fell at your feet. But you were firm.

She wept and wept again.

Firm still.

Goddess', she gasped amidst her breath-struck shaking sobs, 'have you forgot...?'

I never forget'.

Oh listen, dear sweet goddess of the winds, you have forg-, er, overlooked. It is in your praise, greatest of all'.

Kate sang.

"Who has seen the wind?
Neither I nor you:
But when the leaves hang trembling,
The wind is passing through".

'Um', you said, 'well maybe. But needs to be more'.

Kate tried again. She sang to our mortal ears a sweetest sobbing lay,

"Who has seen the wind?
Neither you nor I:
But when the trees bow down their heads,
The wind is passing by".

You spoke then, saying unto Kate

It is good, the song, and so, girl, mark it well. Keep it in your heart and go forth upward onward on your quest'.

I saw Kate's secret winning smile. Then, bowing low, she onward, upward, went.

In the Wind-Blown Clouds

So long, so high she went.

The twists and turns I cannot tell. For you, my goddess, you had hid your head in the sky, pondering your great new panegyric sung by Kate. You had no time to sing of her long wonder-wander-wandering.

But wander she did, and suffered long.

And did not find. For you had blown the clouds around him in the canopy of the sky.

Eden the Garden Place

It was a dream, she knew. She *could* not have lost him and then slumbered soft. And him not found.

But yes she slept.

And awoke. It was indeed al-Yanneh, Eden, the garden place.

A wondrous lovely glade, clear sky above, gentle wind around, blowing with fragrant soughing song of breeze. And dawn with crystal dew upon the grass, last hoar to the winds in sun's new-shine.

She wandered on through many trees, through gentle wind. And soon she came -

Ahh, it was him.

He lay asleep there, breath slow deep and reg-ular.

But troubled too.

Asleep in a steep hill-side, of heather clad and scent of thyme a-waften round about his head.

She looked, entranced. And breath-ed slow and deep, with him.

Ah, if she could take his troubles on herself, bear them herself for him.

But you, dear muse, forbade her it.

Kate could not forbear to touch, a softest touch (goddess, forbid it not, it was of love)

He woke and looked, with sweetest look of love he looked. For her.

Aah, Kate!

Came to, remember-ed himself he did. Backed off with fury, anger, hurt, now the Man-of-Wrath. Away. Away from her.

Stepped back, about to fall a-down the cliff. Be killed again. This time by *her*.

> 'Oh oh, to hold him so he will not fall adown the cliff, is nothing here' cried Kate, oh desperation-ing.

A stick, a knife, anything to hold him, grip, hold on?

Desp'rate, she tugged and tugged and tore, and struggled there, the pain...

But ah she had it now, Fingernail torn from its roots in agony. She fixed it to his coat and held it fast and firm.

And he was saved.

He looked in anger, knowing not. Contempt. For the one who'd ran away from him that time.

He turned away.

By Thomas Cole - The Athenaeum: Home - info - pic, Public Domain, https://commons.wikimedia.org/w/index.php?curid=182975

Oh Wind-es Power

For – who has seen the winds? Yes Kate was right of you, Great Goddess, muse of many minstrel songs, singer celestial of the skies, and... oh and all.

You sang it right oh Kate, for who can see the wind?

But we know it's power.

Think how the winds raise up the surface of the sea and the ships that struggle there.

See how the winds of autumn whirl thistledown round and round upon a road, playing battledore and shuttlecock all at once.

Uplift a terrible great wave, rearing itself up up and up yet more and more as all hold their breath (and all the world as well) up, up above their heads, till it breaks over them and the ship shudders like dry chaff tossed about by a whirlwind, and death stares sailors in the face. The wind that kills.

But when you see full hurri-canes – too wild, too manic, even to describe.

Now sing me true of Kate's ventures midst the winds, rotating storms, low-pressure centres all, low-level atmospheric circulations, spirals of thunderstorms and heaviest rains and squalls and more again.

Thus Kate must learn again of the power of the winds!south-west and all.

Move they then in circles round, whirling to that central clear-some eye, counter clockenwise in the north, clockwise in south, energy through ocean's water recondensed int' clouds and rain as moist air rises, cools, then saturation point.

Next come the circling winds of tropic cyclones fierce, wrought from rotating earth-es mo-mentum, air as air flowing inwards t'ward the world-es axis-way.

Oh Kate, is not our power a thing for amaze-ement? And others otherwhere. But all of strength and devastation to the human life.

Through all must Kate now force her way if she would find him still.

Must go, oh winds, must go mysterious mystic mythic way unknown, to where she knows not where it will be, a-blown by thrusts and gusts must go.

Go on go on go on brave girl to find ...

For thus saith the Lay of Kate and Him.

Above the Earth to Space-ly Heavensome Aire

She was *there!* Was through and up.

Rejoice ye now, rejoice great muse your song is done, for Kate fulfilled.

For as another sang in olden newly time

> "Oh I have slipped the surly bonds of earth,
> And danced the skies on laughter-silvered wings;
> Sunward I've climbed, and joined the tumbling mirth
> Of sun-split clouds, --and done a hundred things
> You have not dreamed of
> Wheeled and soared and swung
> High in the sunlit silence. Hov'ring there
> I've chased the shouting wind along, and flung
> My eager craft through footless halls of air...
> Up, up the long, delirious, burning blue
> I've topped the wind-swept heights with easy grace
> Where never lark or even eagle flew --
> And, while with silent lifting mind I've trod
> The high untrespassed sanctity of space,
> Put out my hand, and touched the face of God".

It was done.

Abandonment

But –

But oh but but –

He had not come.

He'd been below, just there. There by her side, a-ready there. But had not come, he had not come

How could she bear to think of that?

He had not come he had not come.

T' come, had not.

He did not want, he did not dare, he did not love enough.

He did not wish to be there, be there with her.

Ah, that was it,

Ah ah – abandonment!

The utter utter de-solation-ing.

Oh muse, what use is now your Lay of Kate, your honey-tongue-ed sweeten words and golden voice? e'en yours my muse?

For she was desolate, was Kate for him The-Man-Of-Wrath.

For he had abandoned her. Oh Kate, lost there in Space. The end, the end of all. Of all but everlasting pain for aye.

The Poet looked. 'Yes such is life', she said, and lightly took her many-fingered lyre and laughed.

> "Blow, blow, thou winter wind,
> Thou art not so unkind
> As man's ingratitude;
> Thy tooth is not so keen,
> Because thou art not seen,
> Although thy breath be rude.

Heigh-ho! sing heigh-ho! unto the green holly:
Most friendship is feigning, most loving mere folly:

Then, heigh-ho, the holly!
This life is most jolly.

Freeze, freeze, thou bitter sky,
That dost not bite so nigh
As benefits forgot:
Though thou the waters warp,
Thy sting is not so sharp
As friend remembered not.
Heigh-ho! sing heigh-ho! unto the holly".

I cursed her unfeeling glee – but as she turned her back, in haste, I saw her wipe away a tear. A little one. But still.

The Callings

So he had abandoned *her*? But not she *him*. She would go back. What life for her without him there?

Withouten him.

She turned to go, to go back down.

But no! The gravity of that adverse magicked place now held her fast. She struggled, battled, fought and fought again against its clutching winding wind-ing arms. No good.

She could not do it. Relativity, that warring god, had caught her in his power. No good for all she tried.

She cried aloud, and called to him.

Scream echoed rounden heaven, the galaxies, the cosmic universe – the sound of human grief and loss and Roman Virgil's tears in things. Oh there in all, *lacrimae rerum* all..

Hurricane. Earthquake. Maelstrom. Volcano spouting fire to th' upper air, millionfold eruptingness with moltenest burningest lava sent. Airborne from inner earthen fires.

Words cannot tell it, nor will I try.

So now, Kate truly saw her life. Her loves, her hates, her trials and successes too. There by that greater barrier of sound, the sounding winding gate to heaven, to open-ness, to freedom's Aire.

Her dreamen life now passed before her eyes, 'twas there in phoenixsome firesome fearsomen lava, air-enmixed, like she had never known.

> 'Canst thou not help her goddess?'
>
> 'That agony she must undergo', the Poet said with sternness full, 'it is the Song, Decreed'.
>
> 'Great Poet, mercy'.
>
> 'It must be endured'.

Silence of unrelenting there.

> 'But – it is true: beautiful passionate words… They cannot change fell destiny but mayhap soothe the pain? A little bit'.

Thus Kate then spoke, whether to him, to you, to human poetry and human souls, we do not know. But speak she did. In the fullness of her love, only now after all her earlier typhoon blasts completely seen. Now, when it was lost (for such is human life). So yet, she spoke in word-en deeply felt.

Her words struggled, volcano-driven breathed sounds in the molten wind she could not utter but she knew knew knew.

'I am lost. I do not exist, I do not exist withouten him.'

Again the scream bounced on the edges of the universe, the earth, the upper air, all beings now and heretofore. Destroying the universe. Unheard, unearthly too, but all the worse for that. How catch-control what you cannot hear? From hell. Not upper space.

'He does not love me or he would have come. He never did. So you are wrong Great Poet. Do you not hear? *Words* do not help'.

Then came reply in gracious wisdom-words, secret to me, 'Ah but she did not *sing*. The human art, greatest of all the greats'.

Did Kate hear? Mayhap did not. But from somewhere deep within, she *knew*.

She lifted up her voice and sang. That singen calling dear.

With sweetest passionate saddest voice and words she sang. It was for *him* – how could it not be sweet?

And in what venture could such fires erupt but 'n poetrie? But words not of the gentle muses but of furies fell, shrieking Erinyes loud, forced look in the very mirror of her heart. And yet the words, her words of love were sweet, how could they not?

> Oh air, oh wind of my desire
> Breath of my heart, my life
> Spirit deep-set and high
> of my longing
> for finding him.

Fly me with fire
and winging flames of love
to soar me above the earth
and sky
with your breath, my song
For love of him.

And then she call-ed to him straight, in memory sweet, and confidence.

I needed not say I loved you
those years ago,
I need not remind you now
you surely know.

I need not tell you
of joys and tears,
of loves and longing
those centuri'd years.

I did not tell you
in calm or in blow
I was too young
those years ago.

I did not speak
of love and longing
And losing and finding
Ah – but you know.

The goddess looked thoughtful, musing, but my heart leaped up. Winged words like those, and *sung*, would surely bring him now. Ahh, but – a thought:

'He will not hear', I whispered quiet, 'he is outside the world, the universe, this life of hers'.

Kate knew, and she again uplift her voice. And sang.

If I should go

Say only this to him

That as I went I thought of him
That I died loving him.
And that I would wait
There
By the gate of heaven
Till he will come
And we might enter in
As one.

She paused, collecting all her strength ('twas needful too)

If, if
Oh
if
if he should want.
If...'

Her sob reached to the black matter of the skies, broke it to smithereens and shook the stars amidst the sky, their airy wind-sweeped wind-weeped black-holed flights.

'If ...'

He heard. Not with human ears was it that he heard, as mortals hear, but with the antennae of the very soul, the spirit, breath that brings us life, the psyche's inner self. The inspirati-on.

In that wise did he hear (from thee I think it was, Wise Poet of the Aire that sees us all).

She saw again what he had done. He *had* abandoned her. Her whom he secret to himself loved best, whom he had sworn would never never leave. He had not followed her. Oh why!

She did not know, he did not know himself.

Just – he had betray-ed her, that was for sure. She knew. Abandonment. There. There in this lonely place of upper air.

Alone, alone.

Oh he must go after, *he* must go *up*, to her, to where she was. Waiting for him. Disconsolate.

He would, he *would*.

He struggled to his feet. But no way could he go but *down*. No way for his soul to enter there, that secret sacred upper place, barred by the fateful airborn Barrier of Sound.

Well. Well, if not go up he then must find another way.

Go down brave warrior, go you down. And then ...

He floated down. Down down and down. A thousand years.

And then he –

> 'No no not now', said the Poet, 'that is another lay, for another time. Too long for now'.
>
> 'And it is?'
>
> 'The epic hero of many wiles, much pondering wandering 'cross the sea, driven by the storming winds and seagod's angry ire'.
>
> 'Yes yes?'
>
> 'They call him Sinbad, Sailor, others, some, Ulysses name'.
>
> 'The Odyssey! But that, but that...'
>
> 'Yes. So I do not tell it here, that other one. A minstrel I, of many epic lays you know, not one alone'.
>
> 'Yes, but -'

The Poet turned her back, began again to sing. Sweet notes of her many-string-ed windes-toned and air-tuned lyre.

Hush, while she listens not nor looks at me, I will tell it quick (I heard), the tale of him, today.

He fell hard to earth, he did. Lift'd up, oh bleeding all, poor fallen man, to hospital quickly took, amb'lance sirens sounding high and clearly through the air (did she hear it there, far, faint? with shuddering?).

What could he now? Was all prose there. And ordin-ary. So he must be that there too. Humble himself. Disguise his wisdom's wiles.

He begged a porter's job where he was taken to, a fallen man, a hospital. Then begged again on corners of the streets, sold from a market stall, drove taxicabs, then stole, er risked er *gambled,* stocks and

shares in speculationing, and millions' lotteries – hero of many wiles indeed. A degree as engineer, then on.

What do? To get back there. To her. How could he climb? And rise? No bird, no wings to fly to her.

He thought again. Looked t'wards the flying wind-chased clouds, ballooning round and gibbouslike.

Then in his pondering heart from deep within (methinks 'twas you dear muse in quietest gentle voice)

'Balloon! Balloon!'

Build a balloon, he – engineer – could plan, design, construct, could *build*. A great, a greatest air balloon.

Materials where? Ah they were long to find, dear listeners, to cut, collect, to carry there (his lean-to toiling workshop to), so hard and long, a year, 'n then a day. We will not follow now, another lay that is.

Then builden it. Another year. Sing on.

Then – here! Look now!

Cunningly wrought it was, with colours bright above and hanging twisted ropes, basket below of sixfold bamboo canes made such as three great men might go therein. Then was there marvelling all around, and many throngs t' admire its cunningness. Aghast but longing too.

'Oh me? Yes me! Adventurer, let me go along! Yes me!'

But he alone stepped in.

And pray-ed there, that man of art.

'Now to the winds do I commit my soul'.

The Wind

And the winds blew hard and blew again, and – carried him.

And carried him to the many islands in the sky, and many dangers too, and many women lusting after him. But his mind stayed firm. He was Kate's, true. For evermore.

And now at last, at last he was coming near, to that holy upper secret place a-near.

The air-filled heaven.

Far off he saw her. Even in her sadness, she, The-Beautiful-of-Women. There.

He stepped from out, from out the basket of the Great Balloon.

No no he *leaped*.

She stepped across the Barrier to himself. And smiled at him.

In Greek mythology, **Aeolus**, the son of Hippotes, was the ruler of the winds encountered by Odysseus in Homer's *Odyssey*. Aeolus was the king of the island of Aeolia, where he lived with his wife and six sons and six daughters. To ensure safe passage home for Odysseus and his men, Aeolus gave Odysseus a bag containing all the winds, except the gentle west wind. But when almost home, Odysseus' men, thinking the bag contained treasure, opened it and they were all driven by the winds back to Aeolia. The four main anemoi (winds) are **Boreas (North), Zephyrus (West), Notus (South) and Eurus (East)**; their Roman equivalents are, respectively, Aquilo (or Aquilon), Favonius, Auster and Vulturnus.

By Ed Stevenhagen (Overleg) . - from nl.wikipedia Afbeelding:Aeolus1.jpg, Public Domain, https://commons.wikimedia.org/w/index.php?curid=764432

Around Around

The Poet turned around again. She looked at me and smiled.

'Ah are you there? A man of many wiles indeed'.

I nodded guiltily, not knowing how to look, or where ...

'It is not yet the end', she said.

And as she spoke, Kate took the hero's hand to lead him in.

But the Barrier was shut, tight shut against. Locked with a thousand keys it was, each faster than the last. Against-en them.

What can they do? Even the hero of many wiles was stuck. Stuck fast there with his love, outside. Outside the winding wind-en wind-fast mounted walls of heaven.

But not for long.

'Kate', then he said, oh man of wily thoughts, remembering, 'oh my dear love, in that learning of the winds did they every way blow straight ahead? '

'No', said Kate puzzling it, 'they rotate, go round'.'And particles, atoms, molecules, what fashion they? '

'Not sure', said Kate, 'round, I suppose'.

'And the world, the galaxies, the cosmos-universe – are they long, straight, parallel passing or or ...'

'Circles, circular' cried Kate, 'they wind back, back, to where they start, begin. Are – *globular*!'.

'Even so', said the man of cunning thought, 'if we cannot enter in the front we will go round, come by the back, around'.

'Aha, and take them from the rear, behind, back door, the way to heaven', cried Kate.

And so they did. Straightway set off then, round, through long and unrelenting void.

It was not easy, many centuries I think. Ah *you* would know, my goddess muse, if you – hi you! – if listening still (I think you may be in a sulk, thinking I stole your song.

You forget, you, High Poet of the gales and winds, great among greatest – in oral poetry, poets cannot plagiarise).

It was no easy way because the man of many wiles was still a man of wrath. From guilt perhaps f'betraying Kate his love (it is the way). He knew his many many years of toil on th' earth had proved his love. But she? did she know? accept? He was not sure.

So through the darkness of uncharted space, they went.

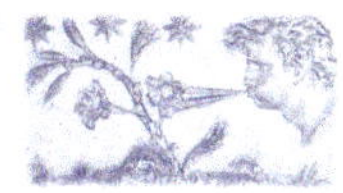

The Unrelenting Void

So on still on they went, he first, Kate follow-following.

'You think the void is empty?' asked the Poet, more friendly now, 'Maybe to mortal eyes. But travel there and you will stumble over crags, halt at Black Matter, circle the flaming stars and dead ones too, encounter fearsome terrifying precipices and cliffs and falls. And cosmic winds that chill the skin and drive to death'.

'Can they survive all that?' I asked, too full of horror to enquire in full.

And so she answered me. 'It is impossible' she said.

Ah Kate. To end like that.

'But with love', whispered the goddess 'all things then are possible'.

And as the poet of olden poets, Persian Rumi, sunni-sang

"My place is placeless,
a trace of the traceless.
Neither body nor soul.

I belong to the beloved,
I have seen the two worlds be as one
and that one call to and know,
first, last,
outer, inner,
only that breath breathing human being".

And so they struggled on, for they were human too.

Th'impossible Unwindable Impassible

Half way by now they were, or nearly so.

So on they go, exhausted now, but no give-up. He first, the hero, she still follow-following him.

Now a great rock lies in their way, a precipice below. Below again the fearsome farthest flames of hell, the central fiery earth-es core, flames ready to leap volcano-wise. Devour them.

Narrow and narrower was the path. Then narrower steeper still. The hero tried it first, staff in his hand.

'Oh careful careful', cried out Kate, 'hold on me'.

He shook his head and ventured on, Kate hid her eyes.

She heard the tumble there, the skirl, the fall, increasing down and down and spiralling down, too young she was to help, too young always in all her lives, Kate-Pearlen epic lives and tales, she could not take it, panicked, eyes that dared not look, but there it was, no help there was, the jangled tangled wangling swangling grinning swirling swinging fall with stones a-hurtle plucked from jangle tangle world aburst with iron glints and sparks like firing stars afall, the jagging sparking iron smith-smelt furnacing that metal melten glowed and hammer-ed to kill him below, oh cannot bear, the sea, too young too loud too tragedy too love too young to ...

The crash.

He had *fallen*.

Far far below she saw him. Oh! He clinging there, small rock projection, fragile crumbling one, slip-slip and slip again, unlocking lock-ed holden-precipice hand, not-holden now and slipping down so slowly-fast.

'*Keep back* Kate', feebling voice, '*Keep back* and save yourself. For me – there's no way up'.

Would Kate have *that*? Not needing Poet's Voice to tell her how. She knew.

She tugged. She tugged. She pulled (oh, worse than fingernail), and then her hair was free, her long hair, all of it, hair that he loved. Free from her scalp.

She plaited it, in haste, in threesome triad twists. Then bit by bit, she let it down.

And up he climbed, rapunzelling. Easy it was. For love.

So then he saw, himself. Easy it was again. That she, that Kate, that she, she truly lov-ed him, had given her hair. Loved after all he'd done, abandoning her.

Deep in his pondering many wile-some loving thoughts, going first, he all but fell. Again. For there before them lay a jagged, deep-cut, cruelling chasm in black-set crag, with fires grinning deep below, gaggling-giggling-grasping-yawning cruel for human prey, a painful traverse-cross 'cross life and death.

And there beyond – the entrance that they sought. At last. The secret back way into heaven.

He leaped, he *leaped*, his long legs made it. Just. Across the chasm.

But Kate, her leap too short, no way for her to cross .

Impasse impassible impossible.

He reach-ed out his arm, no staff had now (lost down the precipice below).

It was too short, ah *just* too short, it did not reach.

Was any hesitation there, my muse?

No. None.

He tore at his coat. And had it off. His jerkin next.

He tore at his arm. Not easy, quick, he tugged and tugged and struggled and hard and mightily. And sore.

And sore sore sore.

'Oh oh Great Poet, stop it there, stop stop, you cannot let him suffer so, no no – '.

'Ah no', she spoke so solemnly, never before I'd heard her so, 'no poet has that power but only God. Who saw his son suffer to death and did not choose to intervene.

'And yes' you went on thoughtfully 'this is perhap indeed and verily. He, only one, 'tis *He*. The sacrifice for love. Once more'.

And now he had it off, torn and teared off.

There was his right arm free, away from shoulder now.

He held it out. Two arms together now, on end, clutched tight, they reached across to her.

He pulled her to his side.

His one arm there enfoldened her.

They walked in through the gate.

In the Beginning Was...

Now in the valley of dry bones sing through the wind, great goddess, sing us de song of de Lawd.

'Nucleus connected to the atom
Atom connected to the molecule
Molecule connected to the million trillion galaxies of multi-universe.
Hear de word of de Lawd'.

And hear again the soft wind's ayre.

'Toe bone connected to the foot bone
Foot bone connected to the heel bone
Heel bone connected to the ankle bone
Ankle bone connected to the shin bone
Shin bone connected to the knee bone
Knee bone connected to the thigh bone
Thigh bone connected to the hip bone
Hip bone connected to the back bone
Back bone connected to the shoulder bone
Shoulder bone connected to the neck bone
Neck bone connected to the head bone
Head bone connected to the hairs, all there,
Hear de word of de Lawd'.

'And – ', said the Poet, 'do not forget – arm bone connected to the shoulder, yes?'
And ah, the miracle, the arm, the breath, first breath, the breathing (hear as it was spoke in ancient times), it was connect, arm to shoulder back again. And

'Hairs connected to de head bone
Head bone to the heart that love
Dem bones, dem bones gonna walk around.
Dem bones, dem bones gonna walk around.
Dem bones, dem bones gonna walk around.
Hear de word of de Lawd'.

And so the story is told. They were together now.

'Twas love.

For evermore.

For in the beginning and the ending was love, the breath of life.

Or mayhap in another way. For oh, dear goddess of the winds, methinks it is the same or like, for are there not other tales, the myths we retell still in mortal times? The magick truths?

Are there not more, to come, we know not yet?

It is the story too of you.

Yourself.

The one that grew through mists and fires and flames and winds of deepest farthest space.

Kate too.

THE PEARL.

***

Thus spake the Poet of Poets to me in the rosy fingered dawn one day, and thus have I transcribed it, faithful, here.

'The Lay of the Lady Catherine and of her Hero deare'

THE END

Ruth

Author's Notes

Prologue

'Sing oh air ….' – Homer's epics, deeply resonant and influential throughout this tale, open with comparable invocations: 'Sing oh goddess …', 'Speak and tell me oh muse…', then after that reverting mainly to the third person, quoting, in a sense, what the muse had sung. Thus the epics are in a way set apart from the ordinary world as if in quotation marks, giving them their mythic and somehow timeless quality.

Oh wind, would it might be so of this my tale – but it is yours – told here.

Chapter 2

Though expressed as Kate's experiences told by the wind, the details are largely taken from my (the author's) memories of my childhood in Donegal (my mother's take on it is given in her enchanting and enchanted memoir *Reaching for the Fruit: Growing up in Ulster* by Agnes Finnegan).

Chapter 3

Wind poems

East – C. A. Morrow

North – Linda Ridge

West – Percy Bysshe Shelley

South – Siegfried Sassoon

Chapter 4

'… perhap another time' – in *The Black Inked Pearl*, Chapter 4

Chapter 6

"Who has seen the wind …" Christina Rossetti.

Chapter 7

"… surly bonds …" from 'High flight', poem by John Gillespie Magee, Jr.

KATE-PEARL BOOKS

Romance novels

The Black inked pearl, a journey of the soul

Pearl of the Seas, a fairytale prequel to The Black Inked Pearl

The helix pearl, the story of the wine-dark garrulous sea

Pearl of the Wind

Fire Pearl. Tale of the Burning Way

Children's

Oh Kate! illustrations by Rachel Backshall (a first nature and counting book)

The magic adventure: Kris and Kate build a boat, with illustrations by Rachel,Backshall (picture book)

Other

Kate's black ink poems

Black Silk Pearl (Rachel Backshall silk art)

"Black ink pearl", a screenplay

Forthcoming

Kate-Pearl romance novels

Pearl of the trees and woods

Ah but thy tears are pearl

Children's

Kris and Kate's next adventure: the magic Pearl-Maran (picture story book)

The enchanted Pearl-Away (chapter book)

Other

The Kate-Pearl colouring book, with Rachel Backshall.

Orpheus with his lyre, in pearls of song and shadow.

HEARING OTHERS' VOICES

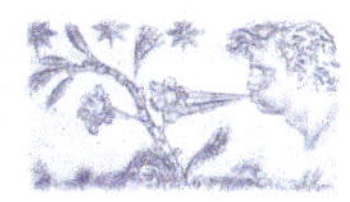

Hearing Others' Voices is a transcultural and inter-disciplinary series edited by anthropologist Ruth Finnegan and others for Callender Press, to inform and engage general readers, under-graduates and, above all, young adults and students to reflect on who and where they are and to explore recent advances in thought, unaccountably overlooked areas of the world, and contemporary key issues.

Each volume is by an acknowledged expert (international authority, fellow of a national academy, professor, or the like, together with the brightest of younger scholars and practitioners) – authors who are eager to communicate outside the too often closed realms of academe. General readers will find much to interest them, set out in straightforward but not simplistic terms. But it is above all to the eager young that the series is directed – the generation who will soon hold our precious earth and its resources and peoples in their hands and be responsible for it.

Less textbooks, more exciting collections for reflection and challenge, the series gives readers a unique route into greater awareness of our wonderful world, far and near, east and west, past and present.

Hearing Others' Voices The HOV logo was created specially for us by the celebrated designer Rob Janoff, creator of the Apple logo.

The first volumes were released in November 2018, preceded by the October launching Chengdu, west China of the Chinese version of Rob Janoff's amazing personal account of how he created the famous apple logo. See Page 60 for latest publications.

I look forward to receiving your ideas, questions, arguments, criticisms and challenges. Let's hear your views, read your poems and see your art and other materials. Photos and videos too, images, and links to music and poetry and thoughts please, your own and others'. The series, after all, is called **Hearing Others' Voices** – yours very much included – so that's what it's all about.

Ruth

ruthhfinnegan.com

RUTH FINNEGAN
OBE FBA FAFS FRAI

Emeritus Professor
The Open University
Anthropologist and
prize winning author

Latest Callender Press and HOV publications

(February 2023).

The Diet and Path of an Amazonian Shaman. Callender Nature 4, January 2023, *Laurent Fontaine.*

Birds and Humans: who are we? Callender Nature 5, January 2023, *David Campbell Callender AKA Ruth Finnegan.*

GRASS: Miracle from the earth. Callender Nature 6, February 2023 (3rd Ed), *David Campbell Callender.*

The Hidden Lives of Taxi Drivers: a question of knowledge, January 2023. Callender Press (also available as an EPUB), *Ruth Finnegan.*

Forthcoming 2023

The Fire Pearl: Tale of the Burning Way,, Callender Press, *Ruth Finnegan.*

Join the Oak Grove Readers and Writers Association on Facebook and get the FREE eBook LISTEN TO THIS.

www.ingramcontent.com/pod-product-compliance
Ingram Content Group UK Ltd.
Pitfield, Milton Keynes, MK11 3LW, UK
UKHW062255290726
14090UKWH00017B/702

9 781739 893705